Why Chameleon Changes Colour

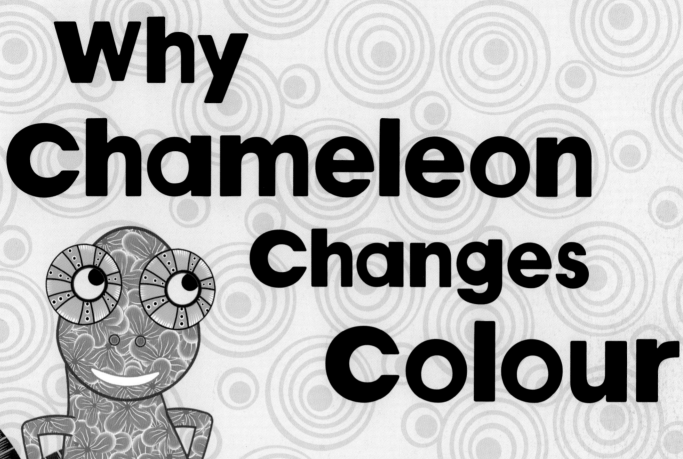

Series created by
Claudia Lloyd

PUFFIN

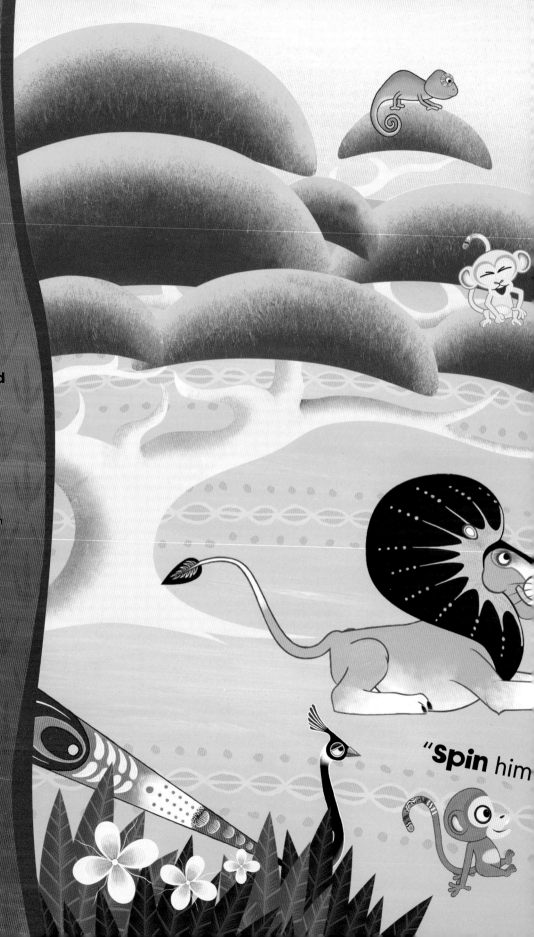

Text based on the script written by Edward Gakuya and Claudia Lloyd.

Illustrations from the TV animation produced by Tiger Aspect Productions Limited and Homeboyz Entertainment Kenya.

PUFFIN BOOKS:
Published by the Penguin Group: London, New York,
Australia, Canada, India, Ireland, New Zealand and South
Africa. Penguin Books Ltd, Registered Offices: 80 Strand, London
WC2R 0RL, England. Published in Puffin Books 2012.

Made and printed in China.

003

ISBN: 978-0-141-33938-2

"**Spin** him

You see there was a time when **Chameleon** wasn't **bright** and **colourful.** Chameleon was very **grey . . .** and even a little bit **dull.**

"What trick shall I do with Tortoise next? **Spin** him? **Flip** him? **Catch** him on my back?"

"**Flip** him! We love **Tinga** tricks!"

"Your turn, Chameleon! Would you like to do a **Tinga trick?**"

"Er . . . **no** thank you."

"**Please**, Chameleon!"

"**Please!**"

"**PLEASE!**"

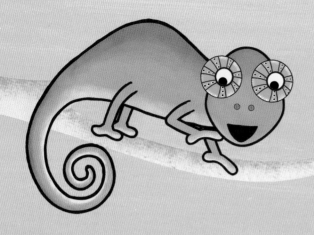

"Oh, all right then," said Chameleon. "I'll do **something.**"

"**Excellent**, Chameleon," said Lion. "We're all looking forward to it!"

"OK, here goes," said Chameleon.

"Now you **see** me . . .

". . . Now you **don't!**"

"But your **tail** is sticking **out!**" said Monkey.

"Oops!"

"Oh dear!"

"Ohhh . . ." sighed Chameleon.
"I'm not very good
at **Tinga tricks.**"

Chameleon wasn't very good at **singing** either. He always **forgot** when to join in . . .

"Your **shin** bone's connected to your **knee** bone . . ."

"Your **knee** bone's connected to your **thigh** bone . . ."

"Your **thigh** bone's connected to your **back** bone . . ."

"Your **back** bone's connected to your **neck** bone . . ."

". . . Chameleon?"

"**Er . . .** Is this the bit where **I** should **sing?**" said Chameleon.

"Oh really, Chameleon," said snooty Peacock. "You are as **grey** and **dreary** as a rainy day."

"No you're not, Chameleon!
You're . . . You're . . . "

**"I'm . . . dull,
boring** and **grey.**
Just like a **rainy day**,"
sighed Chameleon.

"Nonsense," said Lion.
"You are fine just the
way you are."

"Now we must hurry.
The **Big Rains** are coming!
It's time to take shelter.
Wanyama! Animals! Follow me."

The animals took shelter from the rain.
It **rained** and it **rained** and it **rained.**

"Is the rain **ever** going to stop?" asked Elephant.

"It doesn't look like it," said Tortoise.

"I know. Let's play a **game!**"
said Monkey.

"Let's play **Tinga tricks!**"

"We can **spin** Tortoise to
see who should go
first!" said Giraffe.

"Oh no," whispered Chameleon.
"Not more **Tinga tricks!**"

"Tinga tricks, Tinga tricks!"

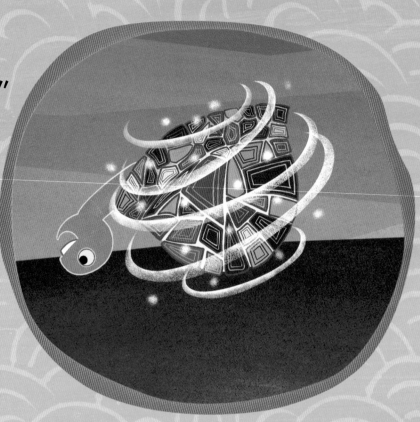

"It's **your** turn, Giraffe!" said Tortoise.

"I can touch my **tail** with my **nose** . . . Look!"

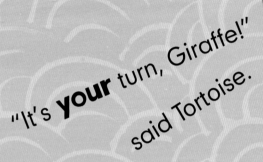

"You **next**, Elephant!" said Monkey.

"What can **you** do?"

"I . . . can . . . **tie my trunk in a knot!**
Let's spin Tortoise again!
Who's next?"

"**Oh dear**," whispered Chameleon.
"Please don't let it be **me!**"

Poor Chameleon was so worried
about **not** having a **Tinga trick**
that, while the animals were busy
playing, he quietly slipped
out of the cave.

Poor Chameleon wandered by himself in the **rain**.

"Why do I have to be **grey?**" sighed Chameleon. "It's true what they say.

Like a **rainy day**, I'm **grey**, just **grey**."

Back in the cave, Tickbird noticed that Chameleon was **missing.**

"**Where** is Chameleon? I thought he came to the cave with us."

"He was **here** a moment ago," said Hippo.

"**No animal** should
be alone in the **Big Rains**,"
said Lion. "Come,
we must **find** him."

So the animals set out to **find** Chameleon.

Chameleon sat alone in the **rain**, but then **Butterfly** fluttered by.

"**Jambo**, Chameleon," said Butterfly. "Why so glum?"

"I'm **grey**, Butterfly. Like a **rainy day**," sighed Chameleon. "I wish I could stand out, like Peacock with his **feathers** or Giraffe with her long **neck**.

And look at **you** with your beautiful, **colourful** wings!"

"I didn't always stand out you know," said Butterfly. "I was a **dull** little caterpillar. But **pole**, **pole** . . . slowly, slowly . . .

good things come to those who wait."

And then all of a sudden . . .

"**Look!**" said Butterfly.

"**A rainbow!**"

"Is that a **rainbow?**"
said Chameleon.

"It sure is!" said Butterfly.
"Have hope, Chameleon.
**Magical things happen
when it rains!**"

"A **rainbow**, wow!" said Chameleon.
"Right here at my feet! I wonder
what would happen if I . . ."

Chameleon dipped his foot in the **rainbow**. **"Orange!** Did my foot go orange?"

"Purple! That was definitely purple. **Woohoo!** I'm not **grey** any more!"

All the animals were still **looking** for Chameleon
when suddenly they heard singing.

"Is that **Chameleon?**" said Giraffe.

"**Singing** and **laughing?**"
said Monkey.

"I do believe it **is!**"
said Lion.

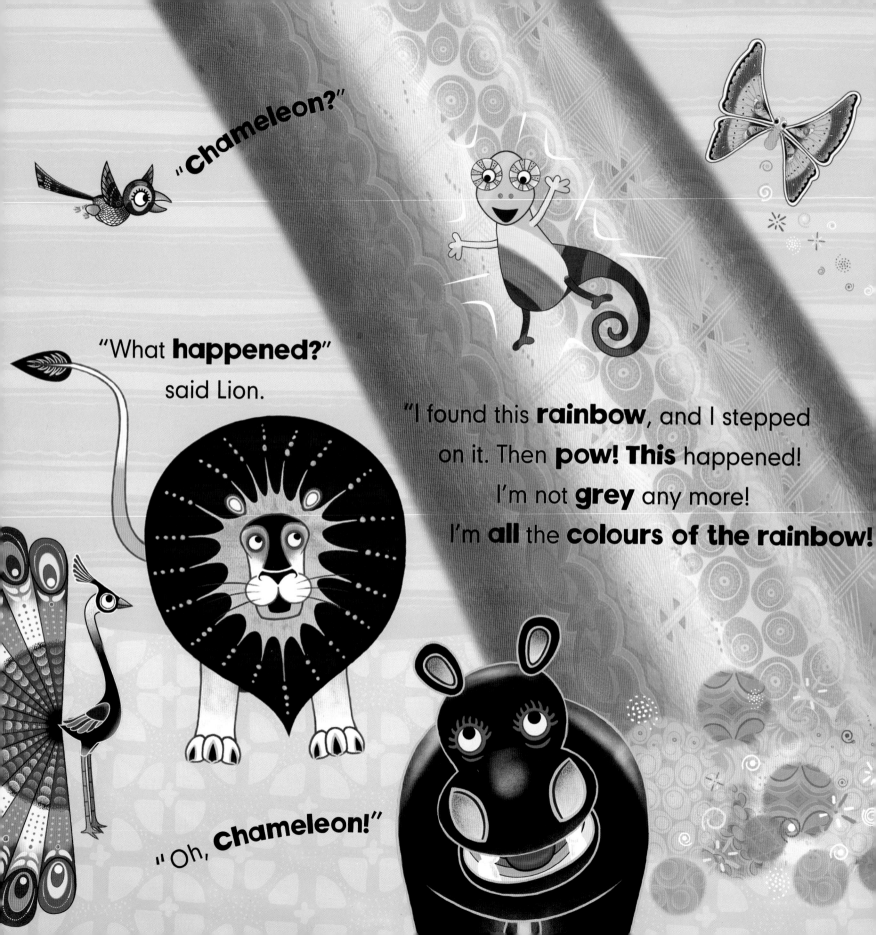

"Chameleon?"

"What **happened?**"
said Lion.

"I found this **rainbow**, and I stepped
on it. Then **pow! This** happened!
I'm not **grey** any more!
I'm **all** the **colours of the rainbow!**

"Oh, **Chameleon!**"

And that's **why Chameleon changes colour!**
He soaked up all the colours of the **rainbow**
and from that day on he became the **master of colour!**

"Can you do **my** colours?"

"TA DA!"

"I told you. **Magical things happen when it rains!**" said Butterfly.